Anna's Christmas Wish

Anna's Christmas Wish

by

Wendy Jones

ISBN: 1-55517-474-4
v.1

Published by Bonneville Books

Distributed by:
925 North Main, Springville, UT 84663 • 801/489-4084

CFI

Publishing and
Distribution Since 1986

Cedar Fort, Incorporated

CFI Distribution • CFI Books • Council Press • Bonneville Books

Typeset by Virginia Reeder
Cover design by Adam Ford
Cover design © 2000 by Lyle Mortimer

Printed in the United States of America

Dedication

To Ben, Megan, Sarah and Andrew,
Love, Mom.

Acknowledgments

Emily Allyn,
for the chapter art.

Chapter 1

Anna stood staring at Emily through the window, just as she had every after-noon for the last two weeks. Her brown curly hair rolled off her shoulders as she set her books down on the sidewalk and stepped closer to Emily. Anna's brown eyes grew wide as she pressed her hands and freckled nose against the window pane.

"Good afternoon Emily," she said, leaving her breath on the cold glass. It was the Monday after Thanksgiving and eight-year-old Anna Green was once again in front of the gift shop window, talking to Emily. Emily was an elegant porcelain doll for sale in the shop's large display window. Her dark brown hair framed her exquisite face with perfect ringlets. Her big green eyes sparkled just like Anna's. She wore a red velvet coat and dress. The coat was trimmed with snow-white fur, and on her head was gently placed a matching fur hat.

Anna closed her eyes and imagined herself having a tea party with Emily. Just as she was about to pour the tea, someone lightly touched her shoulder and a kind voice said, "Hello Anna. Is Santa going to bring you the Emily doll for Christmas?"

"Pardon me?" said Anna, turning to find Mrs. Wellington, the gift shop owner, standing next to her.

"I was wondering if Santa was going to bring you Emily for Christmas?" she repeated. "I've seen you each day after school looking at her through the window.

I know my granddaughter would have loved a doll like this when she was your age." She paused thoughtfully and then continued. "We used to have the most wonderful tea parties together, but she grew up and moved away. I haven't had a tea party in years." Mrs. Wellington's voice drifted off as she thought about the past. "I'm sorry," she said, shaking her head and smiling. "I didn't mean to ramble on. You were going to tell me if Santa was bringing you Emily for Christmas."

The sparkle faded from Anna's eyes as she looked down at her feet and quietly said, "Santa doesn't come to my house."

"What?" asked Mrs. Wellington. "Why wouldn't Santa come to your house?"

"Well," explained Anna as she awkwardly shuffled her feet. "My mom has been sick for a long time and my dad lost his job. He missed too much work taking care of her." Anna paused and looked up wistfully at Mrs. Wellington, "So, Santa probably won't be coming to my house again this year."

"I'm so sorry to hear that," said Mrs.

Wellington, taking Anna by the hand. She knelt down and looked softly into Anna's eyes. "Anna, why don't you come into my shop and warm yourself by the fire before you go home."

"Can I really?" Anna asked as she quickly scooped up her books.

"Of course you can, my dear," laughed Mrs. Wellington as she opened the door. The sweet smell of hot cider greeted Anna as she entered the shop. She followed Mrs. Wellington past shelves of fascinating treasures to the back. There she could feel the warmth from the wood stove and see the glow of its fire. Anna set her books on the floor and sat down in a chair by the stove. She gazed into the flames as Mrs. Wellington stirred the coals.

Grace Wellington was a kind, gray-haired lady, with a gentle voice. She lived above the gift shop and had run it alone for the past fifteen years, since the death of her husband. Her daughter and granddaughter had moved out of Cedar Cove. They rarely came to visit.

Anna Green and her parents lived just

outside Cedar Cove. Their small frame house was nestled in the woods at the foot of the mountains. There wasn't much furniture, but Mr. Green and Anna always kept it neat and clean. Mr. Green provided for his family by working odd jobs around town.

Anna had once enjoyed endless summer afternoons with her mother. They spent many hours having picnics and exploring the woods behind their house. These things were now only a memory for Anna since her mother's illness had progressed. Sadly, the special treatment needed for Mrs. Green was far more expensive than what the humble family could afford.

Anna's mind drifted as she watched the bright colors of the flames dance on the glowing embers. "Can I get you a cup of cider or cocoa?" asked Mrs. Wellington, interrupting the performance. Anna glanced up at the clock.

"I'd better get home" she said, picking up her schoolbooks. "I have to help my mom. Daddy has a job tonight. May I come and talk to Emily tomorrow?" she asked Mrs. Wellington as they walked to the door.

"Of course you can, child," she answered. Mrs. Wellington paused thoughtfully for a moment, and then asked, "Tell me, Anna, do you like to have tea parties?"

"I'm not sure," answered Anna. "I've never had a real tea party before."

"Well then," said Mrs. Wellington, "Would you like to come over for one tomorrow? We could have a tea party just like the kind I used to have with my granddaughter."

"Oh, that would be fun," Anna said excitedly. "I'll have to ask my dad and let you know in the morning. Good-bye, Mrs. Wellington. I'll see you tomorrow," she said as she went through the door. Anna then turned to Emily and whispered, "I'll see you tomorrow, too."

Chapter 2

"Anna, are you awake?" came her father's voice from the kitchen. Anna yawned and rubbed her eyes slowly, as the night's dreams quickly melted away.

"I'm awake, Daddy," Anna said as she drew back the covers. The floor was cold to her bare feet as she stood up. Anna walked to the window and greeted the morning. She stared out her bedroom window at the colorless sky. The first winter's snow had begun to fall. She watched, enchanted, as fat snowflakes gently drifted by the glass to the ground. The golden leaves of fall that covered the earth were slowly fading from view under winter's blanket.

After dressing, Anna went to her closet to find last winter's snow boots. She worked her foot slowly into the worn leather, discovering that she had grown. She worked the other boot on and walked around her room. The boots were tight and worn, but Anna decided that they would do.

Anna gathered her things and hurried into the kitchen. It was small, warm, and filled with love. Her father was cooking oatmeal on the stove and her mother was in bed. "Good morning, Daddy," beamed Anna, as she gave him a hug.

Her father smiled and said, "Good morning, Sunshine. Breakfast will be ready in a minute."

"Daddy?" Anna said, her voice filled with anticipation. "Mrs. Wellington, the gift shop owner, invited me to a tea party today after school. Could I go, please?"

"Mrs. Wellington? Why would Mrs. Wellington invite you to a tea party?"

"Well," Anna said thinking for a moment, "I was at her shop yesterday and she told me about her granddaughter. She said they used to have tea parties together, and I think she misses them."

Mr. Green paused for a moment and then smiled. "I guess it would be all right. But don't stay too long; I'll need your help with dinner tonight."

"Oh, thank you, Daddy," Anna said, throwing her arms around him. He gave her a bowl of warm oatmeal and told her to hurry and eat so she would not be late for school. Anna did just as she was told. After breakfast, she put on her coat and hat, picked up her books, and left for school. Outside the winter's wind was blowing. Anna shivered as delicate snowflakes danced around her. She wrapped her coat tight around her to keep out the cold.

On her way to school, Anna stopped by the gift shop. She greeted Emily in the display window. "Good morning, Emily. I need to go inside and talk to Mrs.

Wellington. I'll be back in a minute." Anna went inside and found Mrs. Wellington at the back of the shop putting on a kettle for peppermint tea. "Good morning, Mrs. Wellington," Anna said with a smile.

"Good morning, Anna. How was your night?"

"It was fine, thank you. My daddy said I can come to your tea party today."

"That's wonderful," said Mrs. Wellington, clasping her hands together.

"Would you like me to come right after school?"

"That would be perfect, Anna. I'll have everything ready. Now hurry off to school, I wouldn't want you to be late on my account."

Mrs. Wellington walked Anna to the door and waved. "Good-bye, Anna, I'll look forward to our party."

"Good-bye, Mrs. Wellington; good-bye, Emily. I'll see you this afternoon," called Anna, as she waved and ran to the school.

At school, Anna impatiently watched the clock. The day seemed to drag on forever. She thought the last bell would never ring. Finally it did, and Anna was out of her seat and through the door before most of the children had time to close their books. All she could think about was getting to the gift shop.

Mrs. Wellington's gift shop was nestled right in the middle of Main Street. A large blue canvas awning stretched over the sidewalk, protecting the townspeople as they peered inside the large display window. Inside the shop, the shelves were filled with curious treasures from all over the world. It was always filled with a marvelous aroma, depending on what Mrs. Wellington had chosen to brew for her customers. On a narrow building across the street from the gift shop, a red and white barber pole turned in its glass case. Mr. Glines, the barber, was always ready with the latest news and stories from all around the town. Down from the barber shop was the old movie house. It was equipped with a stage that hosted dances and meetings, as well as the latest movies from the big city. Between the barber shop and theater was placed the drug store, where, at the old-fashioned ice cream counter, one could get the "best strawberry shakes in the state," according to the owner Mr. Gates. Across the street was the sheriff's office. Sheriff Cook was a big, kind man who cared deeply for his town. On the corner past the sheriff's office was Crosby's Gas Station and Garage.

As Anna rounded the corner by the garage, she could see the city workers decorating Main Street for the holidays. They had already strung the colored lights from lamp post to lamp post, criss-crossing the street. One worker was on a ladder wrapping each lamp post with a golden garland of tinsel. Another worker followed, carefully hanging pine bough wreaths wrapped in red and green ribbon. The aroma of fresh-cut pine filled the air as Mr. Crosby unloaded Christmas trees in the vacant lot next to his gas station.

Anna paused for a moment to absorb the sights and smells of the Christmas season. She then turned and hurried to Mrs. Wellington's.

As Anna drew closer to the gift shop, she could see Emily in her red velvet coat. The coat seemed illuminated with holiday cheer. Arriving at the gift shop, Anna stopped at the window. "How are you today, Emily? I get to go inside for a tea party," she confided. "Maybe Mrs. Wellington will let you come, too."

Mrs. Wellington saw Anna looking in the display window and opened the door to the shop. The smell of peppermint spilled out onto the sidewalk. "Come in, come in, Anna," she said with a warm smile. "I've been waiting for you."

"You look beautiful!" Anna told Mrs. Wellington, admiring her bright red dress.

"Why thank you, Anna. I thought I would dress up for our first tea party."

"Oh," said Anna quietly as she glanced down at her plain blue jumper. "I'm sorry I don't have a dress to dress up in."

"That's okay, Anna, I think you look lovely in anything you wear."

"Really?" Anna said pleased. "Thank you."

Upon entering the shop Anna found

herself immersed in the peppermint. They went to the back of the shop where a table had been placed by the fire. It was set with charming cups and dishes. Delicate pink roses had been hand painted on each one. There was a matching teapot filled with sparkling cider and a plate full of biscuits and cookies. Anna and Mrs. Wellington sat down to have their tea party. "Should we get started?" asked Mrs. Wellington. "Shall I pour or would you like to, Anna?"

"You can pour," Anna said, as her hand traced a rose on the plate. "I've never seen such pretty dishes!"

"Thank you, Anna. They were my mother's. They were given to her on her wedding day. I only use them on special occasions." Anna sat taller in her seat, feeling very important.

"Mrs. Wellington?" asked Anna. "Could Emily come to the tea party?"

"I can't see why not," said Mrs. Wellington. "We should enjoy her company before she is sold. I'll go get her from the window while you set a place for her." Mrs. Wellington carefully removed

Emily from the display window. Anna pulled a stool up to the table and set another place. Mrs. Wellington placed Emily on the stool. Anna held her breath and looked around the table. For a moment, time stood still. Mrs. Wellington had made everything perfect.

"Shall I pour now?" asked Mrs. Wellington.

"Oh, thank you," said Anna. She carefully picked up her teacup and handed it to Mrs. Wellington. She filled the cup and returned it to Anna. Anna slowly sipped from the cup. The cider was cold and sweet and tickled her nose.

Mrs. Wellington cut open a biscuit and covered it with homemade strawberry jam. "Would you care for a biscuit?"

"Yes, please," Anna said, taking the biscuit. Next, she tried a heart-shaped cookie decorated with red sprinkles. It tasted as wonderful as it looked. Mrs. Wellington began telling Anna about Mr. Wellington and the travels they had enjoyed together. Anna told Mrs. Wellington about school. The two ate and drank until Anna thought she would burst.

The afternoon passed too quickly and soon it was time to go. Mrs. Wellington took Anna by the hand and said, "Anna, this was simply wonderful. Do you think your father would let you visit often? I would love to have lots of tea parties."

Anna's eyes widened with delight. "Really?" she said. "I'll ask my dad when I get home and I'll tell you tomorrow."

Anna helped Mrs. Wellington clean up and they carefully placed Emily back on her pedestal in the display window. Mrs. Wellington bent down and hugged Anna. Anna gently kissed her on the cheek. "Thanks again, Mrs. Wellington," she said. "I had a wonderful time. I'll see you tomorrow."

"You're welcome, Anna," said Mrs. Wellington. "I look forward to our next visit." Anna waved good-bye and went out the door. She then turned to Emily, waved good-bye and told her she would see her tomorrow, too.

On her way home, Anna kept thinking about the tea party. She didn't even notice the cold wind blowing in her face. Mr. Green stood waiting for Anna at the door. Anna ran to meet him. She jumped into his waiting arms and gave him a great big kiss. "Thank you, Daddy, for letting me go. I had the most wonderful time. Mrs. Wellington even let Emily come to the party!"

"She did? Who's Emily?"

"Emily is the porcelain doll in the gift shop window. She wants to know if I can come often for tea parties."

"Who, Emily?" asked her father, grinning.

"No silly," Anna said, taking her father's face in the palms of her hands. "Mrs. Wellington."

"Oh, I see."

"Can I, Daddy, please?" Anna pleaded.

"Well," paused Mr. Green, rubbing his chin. "I don't think you should go every day, but I think it would be all right two or three times a week."

"Can I really? Oh, thank you, Daddy," Anna gave her father another kiss. "I love you," she said as she jumped down from his arms. "I'm going to go tell Mommy all about my tea party." Anna opened the door and ran through the front room to the bedroom.

Anna bounded into her mother's bedroom. She hopped up onto the bed and then snuggled under the patchwork quilt with her mother. Anna gently shook her mother. "Mommy," she whispered. "I'm home."

"Hi, sweetie," her mother said softly and smiled. "How was your tea party?"

"It was wonderful!" Anna burst out with delight. "Mrs. Wellington used dishes that used to be her mother's. We had sparkling cider and cookies. She told me about her family. Mr. Wellington was in the Army, so they traveled all over the world. I think she really misses them."

"Did Mrs. Wellington have a good time?" Mrs. Green asked quietly.

"She did," said Anna. "She wants to have lots of tea parties and Daddy said I could go two or three times a week."

"That's nice," said Mrs. Green.

"Mommy? Maybe Mrs. Wellington could come over here sometime so you

18

could have a tea party with us."

"That would be nice," Mrs. Green said softly as she slowly closed her eyes and drifted back to sleep. Anna leaned over, kissed her mother gently on the cheek and quietly left her room, closing the door behind her.

Chapter 3

The morning sun shone bright on the new fallen snow as Anna walked to school. She kept thinking about yesterday's tea party. It was better than the parties she had imagined during her visits with Emily. Anna stopped by the gift shop to talk to Mrs. Wellington. It was decided that they would have their tea parties after school, three times a week. Anna hurried off to school, excited to begin her adventures with Mrs. Wellington.

For the next few weeks Anna went to the gift shop every day after school. Some days she stopped by just to say hello. But three days each week Mrs. Wellington would surprise Anna with wonderful treats and tell her fascinating stories about the different places she had lived. At each party Emily would be their guest of honor.

This particular Friday, Mrs. Wellington had made French pastries in honor of Paris, where she had met Mr. Wellington. At the end of the tea party, Mrs. Wellington announced that Christmas was only two weeks away and she hadn't yet bought a tree. "Anna, would you like to go with me tomorrow and help me pick out my Christmas tree?"

"Oh, could I?" asked Anna eagerly. She had never gone to buy a Christmas tree before.

"Ask your father, and if he says it's all right, meet me here in the morning at ten o'clock."

Anna helped Mrs. Wellington clean up. They placed Emily gently back in the display window. Anna gave Mrs. Wellington a hug good-bye and then blew Emily a kiss. Anna skipped all the way home. She hoped her father would let her go tomorrow and help Mrs. Wellington pick out her Christmas tree.

Anna looked out the window, it was Saturday morning and snow was lightly falling. She watched as the delicate flakes floated in the wind. Her heart was filled with anticipation, her dad had said she could go help Mrs. Wellington pick out her Christmas tree. She put on her coat and hat and went to her mother's room to say good-bye.

"Be good," Mrs. Green said as Anna blew her a kiss from the doorway.

"Obey Mrs. Wellington," Mr. Green reminded her as she kissed him good-bye.

"I will," declared Anna as she ran out the front door.

Anna could see her breath in the crisp morning air. The snow had stopped and the sun was trying to melt away the clouds. Mrs. Wellington was waiting outside the gift shop. She was wearing a bright green dress that, she explained to Anna, had been made "just for picking out Christmas trees." Mrs. Wellington led Anna down Main Street to Crosby's Tree Lot. The scent of pine greeted the pair as they entered. The neatly placed rows of trees looked liked soldiers in a parade. Anna was so excited that she kept running from tree to tree proclaiming that each one was prettier than the one before. "Well, Anna, which one do you think would look best in my shop?" Mrs. Wellington asked.

"This one!" Anna finally announced pointing to a tall, full, Balsam Fir.

"Why do you like this one?" asked Mrs. Wellington.

"Because it looks perfect for decorating."

"Well," said Mrs. Wellington, "then this will be the one. Do you have your Christmas tree, Anna?" she continued.

"Oh no, we won't have a Christmas tree," Anna answered quietly, as she turned toward the fire in the middle of the lot. She slowly went over to warm herself.

The ever-present smile faded from Mrs. Wellington's face as she watched Anna. She slowly walked over to pay for the tree. On her way she spied a little tree standing quite alone in a corner of the lot. "How much for that tree?" she asked Mr. Crosby pointing to the tree in the corner.

"That tree?" he said pointing, "We were just going to burn it. It's too small for a Christmas tree. You can have it for free if you want it."

"Splendid," said Mrs. Wellington. She then arranged for the trees to be delivered.

Mrs. Wellington hummed a quiet tune as she and Anna walked hand in hand down Main Street back toward the shop. Suddenly Mrs. Wellington stopped, turned to Anna and asked, "Anna, could we have our tea party at your house on Monday? I'll bring the treats."

"Really?" said Anna, her face beaming with delight. "That would be great! Then my mom could have a tea party with us!"

"Stop by the shop on your way home from school. Then we can walk together to your house."

"I'll have the house and table all ready," said Anna.

When they arrived at the shop, Anna gave Mrs. Wellington a hug. "Thank you for letting me help you pick out your tree. Maybe I could come over and help you decorate it?"

"That would be nice, maybe we could do it on Tuesday. Now hurry home before you get too cold." Mrs. Wellington waved good-bye as Anna ran down Main Street.

Anna arrived home and told her parents about her adventure picking out just the right Christmas tree for Mrs. Wellington. She asked them about the plans to hold the tea party at their house on Monday. Mrs. Green said it would be fine, and Mr. Green offered to help Anna prepare the house.

Chapter 4

Anna stood for a moment, letting the sun warm her face on the way to Mrs. Wellington's. It was Monday afternoon, and she was filled with anticipation. She and her father had spent the weekend preparing the house so that everything would be perfect for the tea party. Anna was so busy going over the details in her mind that she wasn't paying any attention to where she was going. Anna stopped suddenly when she heard her name.

"Careful, Anna," said a deep voice. Anna looked up. She was about to run into Sheriff Cook.

"Sorry, Sheriff," Anna said, looking down at her feet.

"It's all right Miss Green," he said smiling. "Just try to pay more attention to where you are going."

"I will," promised Anna, as she hurried toward the gift shop. Mrs. Wellington was coming outside just as Anna arrived. "Good afternoon, Mrs. Wellington," Anna said with excitement.

"Good afternoon, Anna," she replied with a smile. "Just let me put up the closed sign and I will be ready to go." She went back into the shop and came out with three bulging sacks.

"What's in all those sacks?" questioned Anna.

"Oh, just the things we'll need for the tea party," she answered. "Here, Anna, you can carry this sack, but you must promise not to look inside, all right?"

"All right," agreed Anna, taking the sack. "Could Emily come with us?"

"No, I don't think that would be a good idea," said Mrs. Wellington. "She will be safer in the window."

"I guess so," said Anna, a little disappointed.

Anna and Mrs. Wellington made their way to Anna's house. They walked past meadows that looked like sparkling fields of diamonds as the sunlight shimmered on the snow. Anna could hear the snow crunching under their feet. She wondered what was in the sack she was carrying. Anna kept her promise and didn't look inside.

As they approached Anna's house, she could see a man at the door talking to her father. It was Mr. Crosby, from the Christmas tree lot. Anna wondered what he was doing at her house. As they got closer, Anna could see Mr. Crosby handing a small Christmas tree to her father, who looked a little bewildered. As Mr. Crosby left, he wished Anna and Mrs. Wellington a very Merry Christmas.

"Daddy, you bought a Christmas tree!" exclaimed Anna.

"No," Mr. Green said, looking a little confused. "Mr. Crosby just brought it over." Mr. Green paused and then looked at Mrs. Wellington. "He said it was a gift from a friend. I wonder who that could be?"

"Well," said Mrs. Wellington, smiling, "I couldn't very well let my favorite tea party companion go without a Christmas tree could I?"

"You bought us a Christmas tree?" asked Anna, turning to Mrs. Wellington.

"Well, I didn't exactly buy it, but I did arrange for it to be delivered."

"Let's get inside out of the cold," Mr. Green suggested as he opened the front door. "Here, Mrs. Wellington, let me help you with those sacks," he offered. Mr. Green then led them into the front room. A modest table was set and a fire warmed the room. Anna's mother was on the couch waiting for them. She looked pale and thin, but was pleased to attend the tea party.

Anna sat on the couch beside her mother. "Mommy, look at the Christmas tree Mrs. Wellington got for us!"

"It's lovely," said Mrs. Green. "It's been a long time since we've had a tree. I wonder where the decorations are."

"Not to worry," said Mrs. Wellington. "I've brought everything we'll need." She then proceeded to empty the sacks. Just as she had promised, she had everything they needed to decorate the small tree. There were lights and small red and green ornaments. There were cranberries and popcorn to string. Mrs. Wellington had even brought a beautiful angel for the top. Mr. Green began by stringing the lights. Mrs. Wellington then placed the ornaments on the tree. Mrs. Green and Anna strung the popcorn and cranberries, and then Anna placed them carefully on the tree. The three ladies made snowflakes from some paper Anna had found. Anna then placed the angel on the top of the tree.

"There, it's done," Anna said, standing back to admire their handiwork. The small tree seemed somehow bigger now. It had been lovingly decorated and placed in front of the window for all to see. "Isn't it beautiful, Mommy?" she asked.

"It's lovely, Sweetheart," said Mrs. Green.

"Are we ready for refreshments?" asked Mrs. Wellington.

"Oh yes, please," answered Anna. "I can't wait to see what wonderful treats you've brought for us."

Anna turned to her mother and said, "Mommy, Mrs. Wellington makes the most delicious treats."

"She does?" Mrs. Green said smiling. "Then I can't wait to taste them."

Mrs. Wellington hummed a cheerful tune as she arranged the holiday treats on a tray. Anna poured juice into a pitcher and placed it on the table.

The small group sat down to have their tea party. They all enjoyed the conversation and treats that Mrs. Wellington had brought.

Mrs. Green became weary from the afternoon's events, so she thanked Mrs. Wellington and returned to bed. Anna and Mr. Green walked Mrs. Wellington to the door. "Thank you for coming," he said shaking her hand. "Anna and her mother haven't spent an afternoon together in a long time."

"It was my pleasure," said Mrs. Wellington smiling. "I get so much joy from Anna's company."

"Daddy?" Anna asked, "Could I walk Mrs. Wellington home?"

"Sure, Honey," said Mr. Green. "But don't stay too late; it will be dark soon."

"Thanks, Daddy," Anna said, as she kissed him good-bye. She took Mrs. Wellington's hand to walk her home.

Chapter 5

The shadows stretched long in the fields as Anna and Mrs. Wellington headed back toward town. "Thank you so much for the tree and tea party," said Anna, as they walked. "I haven't seen my mom that happy in a long time." Mrs. Wellington smiled. "There's one thing I don't understand," continued Anna. "Why did you give us a Christmas tree? I told you Santa doesn't come to my house."

Mrs. Wellington thought for a moment. She stopped, turned to Anna, and said. "You did, Anna, but I was wondering, without a tree to light the way, maybe Santa didn't know he was supposed to come to your house. Now, with a tree shining in your window, maybe Santa will come."

"I sure hope so," sighed Anna.

"Have you told Santa what you would like to get for Christmas?" asked Mrs. Wellington.

"Oh no," said Anna, "I didn't think there was a reason to."

"Well then, it's settled," said Mrs. Wellington taking Anna by the hand. "Santa is over at the drugstore today. You and I will just have to go over there so you can tell him what you would like for Christmas."

Anna nervously followed Mrs. Wellington over to the drug store. There in front of the store sat an older gentleman.

He had a long white beard and wore a red velvet suit with a white furry trim. Several children were already waiting in line to speak to him. Anna hesitantly took her place at the end. She had never spoken to Santa before and wasn't quite sure what she was supposed to say. She listened intently as Santa asked each child what they wanted for Christmas. The first boy asked for a pony. The next girl asked for a doll and buggy. One child wanted a pair of roller skates and another wanted a race car. Soon it was Anna's turn. Her feet wouldn't move. She looked at Mrs. Wellington, who motioned her forward.

Anna slowly walked up to Santa and climbed on his knee. "And what's your name, little girl?" Santa asked in a deep, but tender voice.

"Anna Green," she said quietly.

"And what would you like for Christmas?"

"The Emily doll that's in the gift shop window," Anna said hesitantly. She paused for a moment and looked toward Mrs. Wellington.

"Anna, is there something else you would like for Christmas?" Santa asked.

Anna looked back at Santa and said, "Santa, Emily's not what I want most for Christmas. Do you want to know what I'd really like?"

"Of course I would Anna."

Anna pulled herself up close to Santa's ear and whispered, "What I would really like most in the world for Christmas is for my mommy to get better and for my daddy to get his job back." She sat back down on Santa's knee and looked into his face. "There, that's what I want most for Christmas."

Santa sat still for a moment. He looked down at the ground and then over at Mrs. Wellington, searching for the right words to say. Santa then turned and looked thoughtfully into Anna's eyes, quietly saying, "Oh my dear, sweet child. That's too big a job for Santa. Those are things that Santa can't put under the tree." Santa paused, looking away. He then looked back at Anna and said, "Have you asked God to help you? He is much better at those kinds of Christmas wishes than I am."

"No," said Anna looking down. "My daddy says that God doesn't hear prayers." Anna slowly got down off Santa's knee and then looked up at Santa. "Thank you anyway for listening."

As Anna turned to go, Santa took her arm and gently pulled her back. He placed a candy cane in her hand and said, "Remember Anna, Christmas is about Jesus Christ. He is God's son. You are also a child of God. Maybe a little prayer would help."

Anna walked slowly back to Mrs. Wellington and took her hand. They walked silently back to the gift shop. As they approached the door, Mrs. Wellington finally broke the silence. "Well, what did Santa say?"

"He said he couldn't help me," whispered Anna.

"He said that?" questioned Mrs. Wellington. "What did you ask for?"

"I'd rather not say," whispered Anna. "I need to go. I've already stayed longer than I should have. My daddy will be worried. Thanks again for the tea party and for the tree. I really had a good time."

"I have an idea, Anna," said Mrs. Wellington. "Why don't you ask your parents if you could come over tomorrow and help me decorate my tree?I would love to have your help. Then I could show you the ornaments that I have collected from around the world."

"That would be nice," said Anna. She gave Mrs. Wellington a hug good-bye, and then blew a kiss to Emily.

Tuesday morning was cold and snowy. The snow was now to the top of Anna's boots; she hoped, at least for today, her feet would stay dry. Anna stopped by Mrs. Wellington's shop to say that she could help decorate her tree after school. She then stopped a moment to talk with Emily. Anna blew her a kiss good-bye and headed to school.

After school, Anna put on her coat and hurried to the shop. As she ran, she wondered what kind of wonderful ornaments Mrs. Wellington had. Anna stopped at the display window to give Emily her afternoon greeting, but Emily was not in her usual place. Mrs. Wellington must have moved her into the shop to watch us decorate the tree, thought Anna. She opened the door and went inside.

Anna could see the tree standing in the corner all ready to decorate. Mrs. Wellington was in the back and called out that she would be right there. Anna looked around for Emily, but she was nowhere to be found. "Where's Emily?" called Anna.

"Someone bought her today," came the reply from the back.

"What?" cried Anna, "You sold her? How could you sell Emily? She's my friend."

"I'm sorry, Anna," said Mrs. Wellington as she came out from the back. "An older gentleman came in today and said he knew a special young lady that would just love the doll."

"But how could you sell my friend?" Hot tears filled Anna's eyes.

"I'm sorry Anna," continued Mrs. Wellington, "I thought you understood that the doll was for sale. I was only letting

39

you use her while she was in the shop."

"How could you sell Emily?" was all that Anna could say. The tears were now streaming down her face. Emily was gone. Mrs. Wellington had sold her. "I never want to see you again!" sobbed Anna as she ran out the door.

"Anna, wait, please let me explain." Mrs. Wellington called after her. It was too late. Anna was already half-way down the street.

Chapter 6

The next few days seemed to last forever. There were no tea parties and no visits with Emily. The gray skies seemed to reflect Anna's mood as she slowly walked to and from school. She no longer walked down Main Street. She didn't want to see Mrs. Wellington or the empty display window.

At school, Anna remained silent, as the other children laughed and talked eagerly about what Santa was going to bring them. Anna wished that Christmas would hurry and come, so it would be over. After all, Santa had told her that he couldn't bring her what she wanted.

It was finally two days before Christmas and, as Anna walked home from school, she could hear the cold wind blowing gently through the trees. She stopped to listen and, as she did, the sound became more melodious. It seemed as though the wind was carrying a faint tune. The sound floated down through the branches and surrounded Anna as if it were meant just for her. She stood for a moment and wondered at the enchanting sound. Anna turned and resumed her journey home, but with each step the sound grew louder until heavenly voices could be heard singing in the wind. Anna continued forward until the voices became the tender strains of a hymn being sung. Anna turned around looking for its source. She saw the spires of the church rising above the trees. Anna walked through the trees toward the church. The large front doors were opened allowing Anna to see the green robes of a choir and hear their voices raised in song. She marveled at the large stained glass window which invited the rays of the afternoon sun to shine through its brilliant colors. Anna watched the colors dance as they fell on the white snow below. Nestled in the snow at the foot of the window was a nativity. Each figure had been lovingly carved and painted by hand. Joseph and Mary knelt reverently before the Christ Child. The wise men and shepherds were arranged so that each could pay homage to their king. The manger was placed in the center so that all who passed could see the Son of God. The years of Christmases past were beginning to show in the figures. Their once-bright colors were now faded, but one could still see the reverence in their eyes. Anna studied the scene for a long time, and then slowly approached it.

Anna thought about what Santa had said. Was she a child of God? Could God help her? She walked over to the manger. Anna gazed at the infant's face and felt somehow comforted by the quiet confidence and serenity she could see in his expression. She slowly knelt down in the snow. She had never prayed before, and wasn't quite sure what to say. She closed her eyes, clasped her hands together, and quietly began speaking. "Dear God," she said, then paused to think, or should I say dear Jesus? That's it. "Dear Jesus," she started again, taking a slow, deep breath. "Santa said that maybe you could help me. You see, my mommy has been sick for a very long time and my daddy doesn't have a real job anymore. I know these are big things to ask for but, you're God, right? So if anyone can help me I know that you can." Tears began to run down Anna's cheeks. "I heard Daddy say once that the doctors could help my mommy get well, but we would never have enough money. So please, God, can you help my mommy get well? She's wonderful and I want to play with her again. And my daddy, he's the best daddy in the whole world. I know he's a good worker. You see, he missed a lot of work to take care of my mommy. But if my mommy was well, then he wouldn't have to miss work anymore. I know you must have lots to do, so if you're too busy, I'll understand. Daddy says he doesn't think you hear prayers, but Santa said that you might help me. Well, I guess that's all. Thank you. Love, Anna."

Anna got up from her knees. A cold wind was blowing and it had begun to snow. She was cold and wet. She could see the choir filing out of the church. Anna quickly wiped the tears from her cheeks. She didn't want anyone to see that she had been crying. She pulled her coat tightly around her and quietly slipped away.

Unseen by Anna, the pastor stepped out from behind the nativity wiping away his own tears with a handkerchief. He paused, watching as her small figure faded from view. He then walked slowly around to the manger, knelt down and looked thoughtfully at the Baby Jesus. His kind hand caressed the wood, gently tracing the lines of the infant's face. A determined smile began to form on the pastor's face as he quietly whispered, "God does hear and answer prayers, Anna." He quickly stuffed the handkerchief back in his coat pocket and hurried to catch the last of the departing choir.

Chapter 7

Anna sighed as she put on her night shirt. It was finally Christmas Eve, and her thoughts were drifting back to the church yard. "Are you ready?" her father called, interrupting the thought.

"Ready," she called back. Mr. Green came into her bedroom and tucked Anna into bed, and kissed her goodnight.

"I'm sorry that Santa won't be coming to our house tonight," whispered Mr. Green.

"It's okay, Daddy, I understand. Santa can't bring me what I want anyway." Mr. Green turned out the light and wished Anna happy dreams. Anna closed her eyes, her thoughts returning to the Baby Jesus lying in the manger. Was Santa right? Did God hear her prayers? Anna slowly drifted off to sleep.

Anna slowly opened her eyes as she felt the morning rays gently caressing her cheeks. She tugged at her quilt until it covered her face. As she rolled over to go back to sleep, she realized that something was out of place. She removed the quilt from her face. Her eyes narrowed as they searched her room. Everything was just as she left it the night before. Anna slowly sat up. An old memory began stirring in her mind. She looked around the room again and then realized it was being flooded with a wonderful aroma. It was her mother's special sausage and biscuits. She hadn't smelled that breakfast for a long long time. Her father had said he would never make them because he knew they would never be as good as her mother's. Maybe, because it was Christmas, he had decided to try. Anna put on her robe and went into the kitchen.

"Merry Christmas!" came the greeting from her mother.

"Mommy, what are you doing?" asked Anna. "You should be in bed. Where's Daddy?"

"Don't you remember, Anna? Today is Christmas. Your dad and I wanted to surprise you with your favorite breakfast. Oh, Anna, it has been the most wonderful Christmas morning. Mr. Drummond from the railroad called. He said that the man who had replaced your daddy got a new job. He told your daddy that he could have his old job back, and they even wanted him to come in today for a few hours. So your daddy helped me with breakfast before he left."

"He gets his old job to keep?" asked Anna.

"Yes, to keep," said Mrs. Green. She then continued, "And then, when your daddy left for work, he found a small package on the porch. When he opened it, there was money inside and this note." She gave Anna a hand-written note. Anna sat down at the kitchen table and carefully unfolded the note. Her eyes slowly traced the lines on the paper again and again, growing wider with each pass. She then read the note aloud,

"Dear Anna,

Here is the money you need to make your mommy well. Remember God loves you."

"Do you know where this came from, Anna?" asked her mother.

"It's from Jesus," replied Anna softly.

"Jesus?"

"Yes," said Anna, "I asked Santa to help you and Daddy, but he said he couldn't leave such things under the tree. He said that the job was too big for him and that I should ask God. So I did. I prayed to the Baby Jesus in the church yard, and he heard me."

Tears began to well up in Mrs. Green's eyes. She knelt down next to Anna and looked lovingly into her face and asked. "You prayed for Daddy and me?"

"I did, Mommy. So God sent the

money to help you get better, and he got Daddy his job back, too."

Mrs. Green thought for a moment and then said, "Anna, I'm so happy that you listened to Santa. God must have found someone very special to help answer your prayer." Mrs. Green got up and walked toward the front room.

"Have you looked in the front room yet?" she asked smiling.

"No, why?"

"Well," said Mrs. Green, "when I was in there this morning, I thought I saw a package under the Christmas tree with your name on it."

"Really?" cried Anna as she ran into the front room. There under the tree was a package, neatly wrapped in crisp white paper and bound with a red velvet ribbon. In the ribbon was a tag with Anna's name on it. "She was right!" hollered Anna to her mother.

"Who was right?" asked Mrs. Green.

"Mrs. Wellington! She said that if we put up a Christmas tree, then Santa would come." Anna picked up the package. She slowly turned the package around, carefully examining all four sides.

"Are you going to open it?" Mrs. Green asked.

"I'm afraid to," said Anna quietly. "What if she isn't in there."

"What if who isn't in there?" asked Mrs. Green.

"Emily. What if Emily isn't in there. Someone bought her from the gift shop. What if Santa couldn't find her."

"I see," said Mrs. Green, "Well, since Jesus was able to bring us a miracle, maybe Santa was able to work a little one for you. Go ahead and open the present."

Anna slowly tore back one corner of the paper, then another. Soon she had all the paper off, but all that was revealed was a white box. Anna slowly peeked inside. Her eyes grew wide and she let out a squeal. "It's Emily! Oh, Mommy! Santa brought me Emily! How did he find her?"

Before Mrs. Green could answer, there was a knock at the kitchen door. She went to the door and opened it. It was Mrs. Wellington. "I know that Anna doesn't want to see me," said Mrs. Wellington quietly, "but I'd already gotten these presents for her, so I thought I would just drop them off."

"It's okay," said Mrs. Green. "I think Anna would like to see you. Come in, she's in the front room."

Mrs. Wellington and Mrs. Green went to the front room. "Anna, there's someone here to see you," said Mrs. Green. Anna turned to see who it was.

"Mrs. Wellington, you came!" Anna cried as she ran and threw her arms around her. "I am so glad to see you."

"You are?" said Mrs. Wellington, pleased.

"You were right," said Anna, "Santa came, and he brought me Emily."

"He did?" asked Mrs. Wellington, smiling.

"Yes," said Anna, "and God brought presents, too. Mommy's going to get better, and Daddy got his job back."

"Really?" asked Mrs. Wellington.

"Really!" said Anna. "Santa said God could help me, and he did." Anna paused,

"Mrs. Wellington?" she said softly, "I'm so sorry I got mad at you."

"It's okay, Anna," said Mrs. Wellington. "Here, Anna, I brought these Christmas presents for you. I hope you like them."

"Oh, thank you, Mrs. Wellington," Anna said looking at the large boxes. "Please, wait here just a minute," she said quickly running to her room. Anna returned with a small package wrapped in plain brown paper. She handed it to Mrs. Wellington and shyly said, "I'm sorry this isn't much."

"Anna, you gave me so much these last few weeks. You didn't need to get me anything more." Mrs. Wellington opened the small present. Inside was a delicate white hanky with small red "W" neatly embroidered in one corner. "Oh, thank you, Anna. This is simply lovely. Did you make it?"

"My mommy helped me," Anna said proudly.

Mrs. Wellington handed Anna her presents. Anna opened the first box.

"Mommy, look, boots!" she said excitedly. "These are wonderful. Thank you, Mrs. Wellington."

"You're welcome, Anna," she said. "Now open the other package." It was bigger than the first. Anna quickly opened the second package.

"Oh, Mrs. Wellington it's perfect. Look, Mommy, it's a coat just like Emily's." Anna held up a wonderful winter coat that was red velvet, trimmed with a white fur. "It's beautiful. Thank you so much Mrs. Wellington." Anna gave her a great big hug and whispered in her ear, "I love you, Mrs. Wellington."

"I love you too, Anna."

Mrs. Green turned to Mrs. Wellington, "Won't you join us for breakfast?" she asked. "Mr. Green will be home soon and we would be delighted if you could stay."

"I would love to," said Mrs. Wellington.

"Anna, would you like to walk your father home from work?" asked Mrs. Green.

"Oh yes!" squealed Anna. She quickly

got dressed, put on her new coat and boots, and ran out the door.

As Anna ran down the road she could hear the peal of church bells in the distance. The sound carried clearly in the still morning air. When the church came into view, Anna could see its large doors open, waiting to greet the Christmas worshippers. Anna ran past the doors and into the church yard. Upon hearing footsteps in the snow, the pastor stepped out from the doorway and quietly watched as Anna approached the nativity. She knelt down beside the manger and brushed the new fallen snow from the baby's face. Gently picking up the Baby Jesus, she said, "Thank you, Jesus, for everything. For helping Mommy and Daddy, and especially for my friend, Mrs. Wellington." Anna kissed the baby on the forehead and whispered, "I love you." She carefully laid the baby back in the manger. Anna stood, brushing snow off her knees, and turned to leave. A contented smile came to the pastor's face as he watched Anna skip toward the road.

As Anna left the church yard she could see her father coming up the road. She ran and greeted him with a big hug and kiss. Mr. Green swung her onto his broad shoulders. The two laughed and talked as Mr. Green carried Anna back home to enjoy Christmas breakfast.